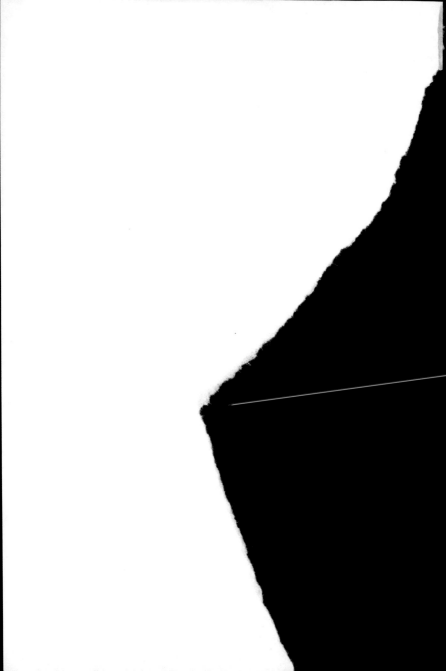

BURIAL

BURIAL

CLAIRE DONATO

TARPAULIN SKY PRESS
GRAFTON, VT
2013

Burial
© 2013 Claire Donato

First Edition, May 2013
Second printing.
ISBN-13: 978-1-939460-01-1
Library of Congress Control Number: 2013932991
Printed and bound in the USA

Cover art:
Patte Loper, "The Sky is Burning, the Sea Aflame"
2010, oil and acrylic on paper, 19" x 23" (framed)
Visit the artist's website at www.patteloper.com

"Can't Help Lovin' Dat Man" (referenced in 'Atrium') was composed by Jerome
Kern (music) and Oscar Hammerstein II (lyrics) in 1927.

"Graveyard Dream Blues" (referenced in 'Atrium') was written and recorded
by Ida Cox in 1923.

Tarpaulin Sky Press
P.O. Box 189
Grafton, Vermont 05146
www.tarpaulinsky.com

For more information on Tarpaulin Sky Press perfect-bound and hand-bound
editions, as well as information regarding distribution, personal orders, and
catalogue requests, please visit our website at www.tarpaulinsky.com.

When you see, the act of seeing has no form—what you see sometimes has form and sometimes doesn't.

— CLARICE LISPECTOR

Now I will wrap my agony inside my pocket-handkerchief. It shall be screwed tight into a ball.

—VIRGINIA WOOLF

These images, however, are hard to get hold of, sunk as they are at the bottom of the alphabet.

— ROSMARIE WALDROP

PREFACE

A morgue is an obtrusive building with a roof and walls, like a house, school, store, or factory. The feeling inside is one of deep intensity, a physical discomfort marked by doubt. Morgue, from the French, is used to describe rooms in early 19th century buildings in Paris where corpses were kept. A corpse is a dead human body; hence your tightening chest, your quickening breath.

A corpse dissected in a laboratory is most often called a cadaver—cremains, if the cadaver is cremated: placed inside a box inside a furnace inside a crematorium. A cadaver is burnt ash, and dried bone fragments are placed in a vat—an urn, to be exact—to be preserved: kept on a shelf for persons to perceive. Now the vat is exposed.

Repeat the expression: *Now the vat is exposed*. Not unlike a small carafe that holds only a few ounces of wine, the urn's translucent vat contains only a handful of ash. To free the urn of its ash—to make room for more ash—persons empty the vat; tap a carpenter's hammer against the cool glass. Wine pours quickly; the glass shatters immediately. Ash blows out of the urn, and the dusty pile of dried bone fragments gathers on the floor. Or, the ash scatters: spreads across a field, over a mountain, into the sea.

You may contemplate, perhaps, what it means to 'scatter ash.' Is it a personal choice, or is it demanded by the dead? To please the dead, should one 'scatter ash'? Each of the five senses may be pierced, and this piercing may be noted, professed. Fingertips smear the bowl of the glass. Oh, the wind blows—does the ash? Sadness draws close. It rests, endures, may never leave. Unless it is thrown up, it may never leave. And the most unpleasant thing is the eyes, lips, and cheeks, which turn green—gaunt and sickly—before sadness is thrown up: issued from the stomach toward the mouth in a low stream.

And thus sadness is thrown up: issued from the stomach toward the mouth in a low stream, which covers the floor. Woe, now the floor is covered. Which is just as well, well with one's soul. Drudgery of mopping the floor will keep everyone out of the room, and there is no advantage in mopping an empty room. It is a hollow task, mopping a room, making it clean, free from dirt and ash. And sadness always sticks. Or, if sadness softens, another sadness hardens in the throat's wooded forest.

Indeed, the throat is a forest: a lush, wooded environment covered in brush, small trees, and shrubs that bloom white leaves. The white leaves scatter; the entire forest is ablaze. And what does it mean to 'be left dead'? At night, one's awareness of death is heightened by the specter of dreams. One's dreams are attuned to the specter of death, death is a ghost, and the ghost's form is fixed: its shape, a body, appears in the mist, is difficult to perceive. Its shape, a body, extends one arm up toward the sky, points a finger. Gradually, a roar of sound descends. The clouds break open: pour cylindrical containers, gallons upon gallons of tears. Tears, fluid content that pours from the eyes to disinfect the eyes, transpire only when the eyes are diseased. Is a ghost ashamed of its tears, its disease? Does the ghost tremble in dreams? Oh, ghost, how your body deforms, becomes so grossly misshapen. Shame is another form of self-destruction, and as the sympathetic nervous system abandons its sympathy, shame grows colder, more sadistic—how wretched, to think! The eye deceives, remains motionless, refusing to see that, like an urn on a shelf or a handful of ashes, a carcass also represents death.

A taxidermy mount is hung above a desk: an animal's body severed from its head. To sever, saw the head and limbs away from the body. Saw the limbs and head away until what remains is a bloody incision, a mangled display, a torso: the trunk of a body that exists apart from its head. 'Get your carcass out of bed,' a person says, and the torso grows—lengthens—and two words—'numb sensation'—are emitted from the head's open mouth. The two words make a knocking sound—'numb sensation'—, and a peculiar clarity comes, takes on the shape of—what is it? A glass? To sit still as glass, to not move or make sound, is to revoke the power of perception: to relinquish clarity, deprive the body of oxygen, to deaden and be dead. Bear in mind, to be dead means no longer to be alive; it implies completely resembling death. And the head of the animal is so round and full. It is the first day of hunting season, and the framework of a body rests across the ground. A deer has been mauled, slaughtered by a hunter for its meat. Admire the victim; pity the hunter. Skin the victim—but the poor creature only wanted to live! And the hunter needs to eat, to devour with insatiable desire. Still, the deer smells dead. It will taste good, grilled as meat. Cooked, the meat will blacken, grow dark in the night like a bruise. So blacken the meat: char its surface with hot flames until its skin turns ebony.

A flower, the seed-bearing part of a plant, consists of reproductive organs, petals, and a stalk, and is typically joined with the end of the deceased's arm beyond the wrist—the hand—before a burial, at a viewing. A viewing is an assembly where a corpse is kept visible, clear, in full view, so that persons of an area or community may pay their last respects, let go the dead. Still, persons never completely let go the dead. A hold is loosened, the knees unlock. Time passes. Persons mourn—show deep sorrow, ceremonial and public. A flower stops living, dies in a hand, and no sooner does death ensue than a person starts to scream, to expel words from her lungs in a dreadful expression of grief. She expels a necklace from her lungs, and no one knows what it means, when it will recede, or how to wear it. No one sees. 'At the open casket viewing, the persons mourned her Father's death,' a person speaks. Another person screams.

Following the end of a life, persons go months without speaking. A person's mouth falls open in an expression of grief, allowing access, passage, or a view into an empty space called the flowerbed, a garden plot where chrysanthemums regenerate by flowering only one type of plant, the chrysanthemum flower. If one fills the deceased's mouth with a bouquet of flowers, the deceased's throat stands in as a vase. Traditional vases are made of glass or china, used as ornament, and stand tall, vertically, in order to support the cut flowers' stalks. Cut flowers breathe more than bouquets; incisions cut along the flowers' stalks allow air—hydrogen and oxygen, smoke and toxins and leaves—to fill the flower from the outside in, giving rise to breath. During burial, the deceased's throat expels air—emits breath—and gives rise to water: a liquid substance that must be drained, must flood out in order to release the body's weight and surface tension. And thus the deceased's mouth falls open, a water duct opens, and chrysanthemum petals cascade. Water floods out from the mouth in a low stream, causing the throat to drain. The throat drains, closes, and becomes translucent. In a supernatural fashion, the landscape that exists within the throat is now perceived: stones, little castles and lines of neatly groomed trees (plastic; covered in algae). A hand presses against the cool glass. The glass shatters; the water floods again; again, the flood is unending—a wholly relentless and torrential overflow, whereafter the bouquet of flowers is dead, and the deceased's body is still dead, and the throat, dead or alive, no longer stands in as a vase. And thus to a great extent the throat is a broken fishbowl, a broken round glass bowl for keeping pet fish, devoid of water.

BURIAL

I

Check-In

Check into the morgue with a bright yellow suitcase,
a bag of dry rice, and a digital camera. Check into
the morgue wearing wild alpaca: drafts of air ring out
in one faint call. Check into the morgue stale from
thinking. Think, 'If TV drones out life, then life must
be dead already,' and, 'If life is dead already, shouldn't
death already know?' Together with frustration, grief
induced by someone else's body's death produces sorrow. In two days—that is, in one multiplied by two
twenty-four-hour intervals of time—Father's casket
will be buried in a grave far away from the sprawl-
ing façade of the city. To this effect, interior concerns
are obsolete. One hears a lever's spring release: gears
rotate outward in a counterclockwise motion. The casket's weight becomes heavy, then the casket descends,
plummets into the ground, and falls through the earth
at a speed that mirrors the speed of a lift, a pulley on
its axis. The speed is steady; the casket is heavy—what,
you may ask, if the mechanism fails? It is widely held
that *fail*, a verb, causes matter to break down—think,

13

'lotus,' think, 'bridle,' think deeply, in silence—*meditat*—from the Latin *meditari*, from a base meaning 'to measure': to ascertain the size of something using an instrument's units. And thus one must bury the dead with the dead's favorite objects, just as one fills a suitcase until it is full to the brim, brimming with objects. Once filled with pebbles, songbooks, rings, and little notes, the casket resembles the suitcase, its bright yellow form. It adjusts to the earth, to the earth's rapid currents, and the rhythm of the currents causes objects to transform into sand. Sand overflows—geysers up from the casket—and forms a beach whereupon a group of funeral-goers stands. Look into the sand; trace an image. A flower, a perfect circle lined with petals, represents the deceased. When one looks into it, does one see the deceased? Or does one see a ghost—the deceased with its eyes, lips, and cheeks out of order? Bear in mind that reflection is in order: constellations form across the beach, and the trumpetfish and cuttlefish all pick at the skeleton's bones, still contained in the casket. The bones are ivory; a whale's ivory, tusk tusk. In an expression of boredom, one funeral-goer yawns, which causes another to yawn. Soon, the entire populace is yawning, unable to recognize the weight of the ghost, the deceased. The perfect circle lined with petals remains in the sand, and the sky is still blue, clear and visible. The sand expands across the beach in one clean, sweeping motion. Life is the body of death.

Repeat the expression: *Life is the body of death.* 'Morgue,' borrowed from the French, is a mortuary: a hard and insensitive building where dead bodies are kept, where mourners gather following death. But from what does a morgue borrow its form? To whom does it owe a debt? Say 'morgue.' The word is a trap. It wreaks havoc upon the brain, the mind and language. And a body rests across a table, concealed by tissue wrap. Its head is severed: Its brain, a gumball, rolls. A coin is inserted; the silver knob, spun; and the gumball is released, glides freely down a chute until it rests in the palm of your hand. Thus the brain is chewed; a gumball is chewed. Images arrive, open and flash, and the mind's eye cannot rest itself atop the image or its contours. Rest closes the hand's clammy palm; following autopsy, the head is stitched shut. And what does it mean to laugh at this horrible sight? Incited when the body is in shock, laughter draws emphasis away from the eye's fixture on the lesion. No, a brain is not a gumball; nor is a head a toy to be opened and stuffed. Shock, which dons the guise of laughter, pollutes the body, is cacophonous. Disassociation hugs the mind, and it is impossible to call attention to the morgue without describing its scenery. Its carpet is baroque. Beneath it rests a colony of dirigible ants that, regardless of the season, steers together. During the rainy season, the ants steer together, wander through corridors in search of sugar, syrup, honey. In summer, a tidal wave overturns the beach; one finds oneself lost in loops: designs that are brightly colored, however colorless: loop loop. One cannot get lost in carpet without being thrown for a loop, a vortex, a swirling eddy, and so many things to call to attention: the antique mantle, painted white; the countertop, marble, cool to the touch; hardwood banisters that loop and climb the staircase, then spiral down from the brain's never-ending collection of rocks. And think—a collection of rocks under waves is a symbol of thought, ever circular, which loops until emotion undulates, crescendos through the body until it reaches climax, at which point it becomes infected, rots. In its irrational display, emotion rots, and 'Father, dear Father, sometimes I'm drawn to the grand hotel'; sometimes the morgue blackens, and its carpet blackens, and coffee stirred with milk is so lightly colored, 'I cannot drink it.' To drink would only aggravate emotion, and every time the hands are placed around a cup, coffee is consumed, causing the brain's waves to accelerate. The brain accelerates, the heart accelerates, the legs, eyes, and mind all accelerate in their various stages of existence; which is to say, the bouquet of flowers dries up. The fish is dry too, though its skin is intact. Its skin may yield to the touch, but won't spring back: only forward, the direction in which the mind must eventually move. Move forward, the mind must, so that the legs, the eyes, and the heart may all move forward too; otherwise, the heart is a chestnut: a hard, brown nut that is impossible to crack. And thus a person looks

16

into a mirror, a surface in a building where the boughs move to and fro in jeopardy. To bring the chestnut back to speed, add a little fire to the gasoline. Fire is liquid; gasoline is bright blue. To terminate the brain's accelerated waves, the body is hung upside-down, whereupon the body becomes dizzy and throws up. As expected, the body throws up, the coffee is thrown up, and a forest is exposed: a beach, a graveyard whereupon the group of funeral-goers stands. Still, to stand the true exposure of an image, part the ferns and split away the fronds—think, 'persons,' think, 'ashes,' think, 'further'—and further and further and further, away, dear Father, an answer forms . . .

Privacy

There is no privacy in the morgue.

Float along the swimming bath's edge, where tall lamps cast pools of light over the water. No, that can't be right. Orange is a light; sky is a color. Tall and drifting on a clear day isn't how . . .

There's no limit to the ways clothing can suit you. Suit up, dive into water. Feel guilt, mostly. Or don't; feel grief. Guilt is the color of sand, and grief is the color of water. Father had piercing blue eyes; his eyes were the color of grief. And the swimming bath's grief is bright blue. The edge of the pool forms a border around it. The border is enclosed. In the pool, snakes encroach. Oh, snakes are so hungry. And the pool is cold. Father was cold too. But he was not cold when he died. He was incognizant. Poor Father. He mocked language, fiction, and poetry. 'Write this down for your book,' he would say, raising his instrument, his voice. Then he would draw back. Then he would inch forward. 'Your damned cheerfulness has always dis-graced me,' he would say. 'I'm going to teach you a lesson.' And always a lesson ensued. Behold, it came to pass, Father was a man. He taught lessons in his language, and also raised his voice. 'A lovely day to go fishing,' he said. 'The water is frozen,' he said. Then he drowned in the lake.

Talk Show Host stands in front of an audience, holding a tray. 'You're going to your high school dance. Would you like it if we gave you a makeover?' Talk Show Host's mouth forms words. Her head rolls from side to side as she speaks, bobs up, around and down above her shoulders. Her hair is the color of sand. Her lips, bright pomegranate. Groundskeeper mops the bath's terrace, flips the stations. 'Due to the graphic nature of today's show,' commercial break, 'a dog at-tacks an entire union of workers,' commercial break, 'a league of tennis players is devastated.'

'It's unusual for a dog to bite its owner's wrists,' Groundskeeper says. Now Talk Show Host looks an-noyed, red and inflamed. Now Groundskeeper's eyes narrow down into water, the ocean's floor, a surface. 'I cannot stand,' she says. 'Feet don't touch.' Against the floor, two feet touch, and a body stands tall, upright, measuring a specified distance from head to spine, spine to toes. Belly-up, the body floats. Belly-down, it becomes a measuring worm: a worm that moves backward and forward by arching and straightening, a straightening arch. Two legs tuck back, kick out and sweep in a circle. Two arms hang motionless, limp. 'It's a wonder the body moves forward at all,' Groundskeeper says, lighting a match. Now a match is lit, the pool is alight, and water is so thin and impure, 'I cannot drink it.' The throat is too thirsty, too dry and too baked. To filter the water, pour it out into a little lake; let the bugs and smoke strain out, bob up toward the surface of the water, which, upon investigation, is filthy, covered in sludge. Alas, the pool is sludge-covered. And bugs are all snow-covered in their shells, washed up on the beach like dead turtles. A beach is a frozen scene too: white sand, white snow, white fish coat the surface of the water. Ice is not sand, however 'blue blue.'

Held up by a lifted chair, a lifeguard waits for a tsunami. 'It will envelop,' he says. 'It will envelop the dream.' Or, it will envelop sleep, the dream in which a tsunami comes, escorting a crisis. High waves greet the dream—'hello'—and the long sea envelops the surface of the mind; at once, the mind's shape takes on the form of a dream, a tsunami-shaped crisis that opens its mouth, which widens, engulfs. 'Hello,' the mouth pronounces, and crisis clearly engulfs the hotel made of crystal language, which wraps around itself in a loop, allowing the tsunami to be seen from every angle, etcetera: loop loop. At night, dreams engulf everything in sight: the hotel, morgue and graveyard all appear and disappear in one clean wide field of vision, and all the little bugs are dead, their corpses carried away by the wave, which floats forward. A mass of human corpses float forward too, singing 'alleluia' in chorus—though only a little, a bit—'allelu.' Before they reach the grand hotel, they crash against the brain's thin bones. Glass shatters immediately; the heart's cool chamber slams shut. Now the eyes, ears, and brain all sense the heart in total crisis, passing away from the chest toward the throat in the pitch of a scream. Now, a person is screaming. Now, a person is weeping. Now, a person is thinking two things, two things—she thinks, she thinks—and these two things take up space in her brain:

She thinks, 'Help.'

Thinks, 'I've drowned.'

Hand Signals

So much is conveyed through gestures, hand signals. Groundskeeper carries a bright yellow bucket, wipes the floor on her knees. The floor is carpet. Her bones are knees. She knocks on the door. 'Housekeeping,' she says. 'Have you stayed in this cooler before?'

Say, 'I'm from out of town.'

A town is an area or surface that lengthens according to the rhythm of the earth. The morgue—the uncooperative, gunmetal morgue—is immobile, flat, and unmoved by the earth, which spins on its axis, keeping its eye on the clock. Since Father's death, the clock's hands have gone stiff; yet the body keeps sounding—*tick-tick-tick*, *tick-tick-tick*—and the phone is always ringing, it's obsessive—the phone is always ringing, never stops; it's a loop. And the brain remains unfaithful to its own magnetic loop: no longer its own boss, its nervous hub of senses must dissolve from time-to-time: the brain must excrete lava; the body must erupt.

Stretched out into its vast expanse, the body's clock sounds *tick-tick-tick*, which aggravates the brain's soft nervous tissue. *Tick-tick-tick*, the body's clock, clock strikes half past ten. *Tick-tick-tick*—the body's clock—the brain—dries up again. 'Turn off the alarm,' the brain drones. 'Turn off the alarm,' the brain tolls. 'Turn off the alarm,' the brain crows, and from the din comes solitude—self-inflicted loneliness—a state of dull repose.

'Where are you from?' Groundskeeper says, wiping the floor.

Say, 'California.' Still wiping.

'That's very far away.'

A window opens. Who opened the window? Behind Groundskeeper is a sign: HOTEL RULES. Juicy fruits, such as watermelons and plums, are not allowed. Pets are not allowed. Drinking excessively, making excessive noise, is not allowed. Highly flammable, explosive, radioactive articles must be registered at the front desk and shall not remain in the autopsy coolers beyond eleven p.m. Breakfast is served from six to nine a.m. Coffee is always served. And what does it mean to 'make oneself available'? Following death, cards arrive. Saliva moistens glue. And it is cumbersome to express sympathy, to compose a little note that says, 'I'm sorry,' 'so sorry,' and 'thinking of you during this difficult time.' Nothing is settled. Nothing is fixed. To lie on a bed, whisper 'shh' . . . That settles something. Soon, grief sinks in. Two eyes settle shut. In time, they re-open: blue, crystal-clear, and enigmatic.

Say, 'I'm going to take a walk,' and Groundskeeper says, 'How long will it take?' The clock on the stand reads seven o'clock. How long will it take? Say, 'Not long, I'm living here,' eyeing the clock. Breakfast is served. The clock's numbers are blue. Groundskeeper smiles. 'I'm living here too,' she says, revealing her weapon, her black tooth. 'Before I worked, I lived at home,' she says, and Apparition passes through her, carrying a plate. Say, 'Did you like it?' Scent of butter substitute, coffee, runny eggs.

'Sometimes,' Groundskeeper says, 'I liked to take walks.'

She stands on her feet. 'I lived near a pond. There was a hill overlooking the woods. The pond was full of fish. The woods were filled with trees. I liked to sit and do nothing. I liked to look at the trees. My husband liked to fish. Sometimes, I swam in the pond. If you open your eyes underwater, you see fish. You smell bait, and you see hooks. And you see fish. Some are rainbow trout. Others are beige. Did you know fish are omnivorous? They don't like to live alone.' Groundskeeper pauses. 'My house always felt like a home.'

Now the sun is shining, lifting up little flecks of dust that drift in and out of the light. Now the light drifts with them, is drawn out, and therein dwells the sounds of water running, running footsteps. And think—the brain is focused on so many things: the shape of the deceased in the carpet's baroque ornament; the feelings that run through the gut while the brain is asleep and, more consciously, the clock on the stand, which plays music. You can control the time, but you can't control the volume of the music. Clamor is white, pink, or brown. Heart cracks the spine like a book. And all colors fuse, depend on one another to form the emotion's continuous drone, which hums only one note in the brain, one lingering pitch. How pathetic, this soundtrack. How unpleasant, its fog, its dually obscure and conspicuous thick. And how ugly, its noise, its absence of music, its sharp, prolonged din in the brain—*zz-zz-zz*, *buzz-buzz-buzz*—throughout which Groundskeeper adjusts the clock's knob, hums a song to herself. 'La-di-da,' she intones. 'La di-da,' she belts out. 'La-di-da,' she hums softly, the song humming itself.

Apparition zooms into and out of the picture, tightens and loosens a lens. Groundskeeper sighs. 'Oh, isn't it a pity, a wholly damned shame? No sedation will inhibit him while he's following a line, he follows one or two.' Count, 'One, line, line, two.' Think, 'One, two, three, four,' and regard Apparition's sustained tunnel vision, his forceful, intent look. Think, 'What an ugly look,' and Groundskeeper furrows her brow, slowly decomposes. Apparition pays little regard. Abandons his subject. Wheels the camera toward the bright yellow bucket, focuses in. Now the lens picks up Groundkeeper's tooth, black to the eye, after which film unravels. 'I'm sorry,' Apparition says—'so sorry,' and, 'thinking of you during this difficult time.' But from his presence, it's obvious: he is shooting a picture. In the morgue's secluded hallways, he takes notes. His presence, a grief staff, provides a small buffer, a form of relief from the decomposing body's broken bones.

There are so many books, the heart reads. So many sentences break. 'Fear is dormant,' one sentence slumbers, and, when it awakens, Apparition, ever-present, will be there to meet it, to feel it, to dull it with his scepter, ornamental and cool as a plum.

And thus a door shuts; again, a lid closes. One lens remains open: grief, the hollow layer of the heart that delineates the distance between reasoning and space, spatial order versus *a priori* sadness, which rustles the natural world like a twister or violent rain; which impairs, sobs, and shouts, and can scarcely explain the basis of its graceless origins. Meanwhile, the body remains disconnected from itself, invalidating the mind, which lacks logic. And in the mind's place rests a fantastic little book—a written treatise bound with thread, tangled narrative strands that make clear what is sensed in the heart is an absolute mess. Yes. Mind's a confused, tangled skein. All on its own, the body-book transcribes thoughts into speech—yarn spun out of rambling shoots—and words once expressed in the mind now take on physical shape in the form of black type: rich, letterpressed symbols that cover his body in formal attire: funeral clothing that, following the burial, will take on the form of a trace in the mind, which depends upon the throat's black hole to make known its duress. Sadness leaves the body dumb. Still in the autopsy chamber, his body waits, undressed.

The Body Dumb

Sadness leaves the body dumb. Again, the mind turns toward itself: one lukewarm rupture of protuberance devolves the back of the head, and the brain expands, implodes, and then refills with helium, which turns memory grey, grey as the overcast sky or a handful of ash, and the hand—the disembodied hand—is severed at its wrist.

Four nerves travel into the hand as Four Men travel into the space. The morgue, which blends into its landscape, is located upon less-traveled terrain nearby the town's periphery: a dull world without color that can only be seen through the eyes of the dead, a hall of minerals. Black walls reflect light, an entire spectrum of bands. As the mind composes, nerves move through the carpal tunnel where, at lightning speed, the brain transcribes the hand.

'Alas,' the hand's bones say. 'The hand must now be dead.' And two words—'numb sensation'—radiate through a person's head like light through glass, echo through the mind as sound, one form of energy. 'Numb sensation'—these words drift through the morgue as do Four Men, and it's true: The mind that speaks no words unlocks language in its depths. Without uttering a sound, the brain becomes compressed, and language is released, flows freely in the mind. Grief floats to the tips of one's fingers—a kinetic place of rest, a lovely place to die. Four nerves pinch up; the sea-breeze picks up; and two eyes look up, roll back into the head. What does it mean to be dead?

Repeat the question: *What does it mean to be dead?* In the beginning, there was a body. Its bones, flesh, and organs were intact, well behaved in all manners consistent with being diplomatic and sensitive, humble and keen to defer to the heart—the nervous heart that falls ill each time it meets his blue eyes' expressionless gaze, his skin's icy, unnatural sheen. And the doe—the poor, female doe—collapsed at the scene. Two cracks rang out. He shot her. He shot her dead. 'A lovely day to go fishing,' he said, yet before he could indulge in his reward—field dress the damn deer and pay tribute to his success, his all-time best, grand aptitude for chase—he drowned in the lake.

Groundskeeper moves through the space. Her expression is gunpowder, no bullets in place. What happened? Why does the mind not remember his face, his peculiar surface, the fine-grained metamorphic rock upon which language is engraved—R.I.P., rest in place against the backdrop of bright flowers in the sun. And the mind—the flowering mind—keeps replacing his image with that of a stone bearing only his name and two dates. Reads the former: 'DEAR FATHER—'. Reads the latter: xxxx – xxxx. Say to Father: 'In my mind, my blue light, is a window that overlooks the lake. I press my hand against the pane, look down, but cannot see the surface of the water; I only see your grave. I close my eyes: a harsh wind stirs my body and, for a moment, my mind is frozen stiff.'

'I run my hand along the surface of my mind to stir the wind, to wake my mind, to impress the lake upon my mind—my half-dead, frozen mind—when at once a doorbell rings; my head aches from the sound; and a necklace of language forms on the ceiling. A sparrow falls through the mind in no hurry. During the night, it is blown from its nest, and today, in this text,'—in this morgue, in the navy blue light of your death—'I cannot read what it says.' Nor is it fruitful to decipher each symbol using the brain's clever finger, which regards everything with inexplicable flatness—even the landscape, devoid of depth. Water seemed shallow, the police report said. The lake must have frozen in stages. And to remember—to trace the mind back to that night and repeat . . . Darkness encroaches, seizes the brain's every crevice, and becomes trapped inside cognition's toolbox, without which the mind cannot formulate a sentence—not even a fragment, no meaningful language at all. To the casual eye, the mind still functions, and the face consists of all its corresponding parts, which descend in their logical manner: eyes, nose, mouth, chin. Again, in no order: nose, chin, mouth, face. Carbon copy. Doppelgänger. Spitting image. His dead ringer.

Groundskeeper kneels beside her bright yellow bucket, wipes the floor on her knees. 'La-di-da,' she intones, and her voice's dull pitch enters the mind as a musical score, a leitmotif the eye, brain, and heart perceive as chattering teeth, frostbitten hands. A band of sun warms the lake, it's impossibly frozen—a band of warm sun melts the lake, 'la-di-da,' melts his life—*tick-tick-tick*—and, at the end of his life, Father was frostbitten too; he was, he was, he was.

Must everything mean several things at once? 'La-di-da,' Groundskeeper hums; the radiator hums; and a flurry of images hum in the brain, answering 'yes.' And yes—of course, indeed—an expression or sound must always mean multiple things. For example, Groundskeeper's voice is the most spacious in the morgue, pristine with clean sheets, fresh towels, trash bags, and little mints. And the morgue—the uncooperative, gunmetal morgue—may be two places at once.

Say to Groundskeeper, 'Do they feed you here?' Say, 'Do you eat meat?' Bear in mind, there are so many things to say. For example, the morgue is historic. It was erected in the 1800s, then shut down for a time. Will it ever close? Apparition doesn't think so. His grief staff seems comfortable too. At night, they make sounds: they shout and laugh and moan and break glass bottles. They knock on doors—knock-knock, who's there? Who could have prevented his death? 'One bottle of wine,' grief staff says. 'Make it two.' And when the wine arrives, they drink themselves to death—to the death—until they cannot tell the difference between drunkenness and death, or until their debauch bothers everyone to death.

Groundskeeper stands. 'I was vegetarian once,' she says. 'Then I talked to a psychic healer who told me I should eat meat. Three times a day, five days a week. That didn't last long.'

That didn't last long. The sun shone, lifting dust. Now everything is grey again; again, the room's walls make white the mind, the mind white like an egg. Say, 'Vegetarianism is unhealthy.' Say, 'Most diets are.' Welcome the rain.

'You're thin,' Groundskeeper says. But from the expression on her face, it appears she has no idea what to say. Truth is, mind never knows what to say, never fully comprehends the language locked inside it. And the disembodied hand serves no use: with one nerve's cessation of its travels through the wrist, each finger takes one final breath.

And thus the transcription of words from the mind to the page is interrupted; this text is interrupted; and a life is interrupted by its body's little death. Sooner or later, what remains to be said will be said, and only rain shall free a body from its mind; only the brain will remain caught in the heat of the room and the room's conversation, which, at an angle, becomes emerald, bright green. Wholly unable to let go the dead, mind always longs to know more, longs to be flooded by a downpour of details that are always withheld in the end, buried alongside the dead in a bright yellow suitcase that, upon further inspection, is completely empty, its contents made bare by invisible hands. Has nothing physical form? Groundskeeper seems to think so, eyeing the body with her gaze, her shallow perspective. Say, 'I have scarcely been eating; my Father just died,' and a wave of shame cascades through the body. To fall back on the dead as an excuse is a dreadful mistake.

Four Men

Four Men are kept in the autopsy room, locked in a cooler where bodies are turned into ice. In the autopsy room, ice is a tempo, a briskness that casts shadows as it melts, an apparition always ghostlike in the chamber, a dead cadaver. Father's cadaver is at rest, half-dead, though very much alive and not yet buried. And thus too the cadaver in the chamber: Its neck and back and shoulders cast long shadows in the lobby, glow.

Morgue guests check into their autopsy coolers to vomit. On an airplane, one vomits in an airsickness bag, a complementary receptacle. When one thinks of lunch, one throws up. Or, a conjunction, offers an alternative. A cup of coffee or a chestnut? A dry bouquet or empty vase? Is your mind unable to conceive of its grief, or has it accepted its waves? Scent of an airsickness bag filled with questions, doubts in life that persons see but cannot hear. To hear the mind's questions, one must first acknowledge there exists no psychic dwell inside the mind, no cognizance. 'Press * at any time to speak with the front desk,' a voice says—is the sound a hallucination, a false impression in the brain? Floating through the morgue's dank halls, a little soundtrack plays. Piano, flute, and voices sing 'ooh, ooh, ooh' in unison. 'Ooh, ooh, ooh,' the voices sing, and the little soundtrack plays. Captured on film, the soundtrack plays, and a body floats through space. Morning comes. A person wakes. On display in the room is a painting: a water lily covered in raindrops after the rain. The water lily floats; a human body floats. To float through the morgue, close your eyes: picture a tall, winding staircase, an endless strip of tape.

Skylight is stained, covered in glass. Images radiate light in stained glass, and the water lily descends its canvas, where there is the premonition of some one, very dead thing. Oh, 'Father, dear Father, is your ghost still at rest, half-dead, though very much alive and yet no longer? Or do the Four Men call out?' (Father, this question scarcely seems sufficient—how might the Four Men call out when 'I have not met them; I have not met the Four Men'?) 'I have encountered Four Men,' remember him writing, 'though I have not met them,' remember him writing, 'I am writing you this letter atop an antique wooden desk.' Remember his handwriting, his exquisite nervous loops: a little 'i' written in cursive, connected to the letter 'n': 'in, in,' 'n, n,' loop, loop. And remember his hand, closed into a fist, performing a small exorcism to rid the room of ghosts. Think, 'The heart consists of bits,' pieces of fish, and then visualize the heart—the cold heart: a sentence parsed into words by the mind, brain, and body—deep, narrow ravines cut off at the stems. What is the meaning of death? 'The water is frozen,' he said, and it happened fast—the deer appeared, stood gracefully atop the ice and lengthened her lean neck. He shot her. He shot her dead. And then he too sank down, dead, exhausted from the ice and drift and questions: Is death immediate, or does language postpone absence with two fists? And it is curious that the heart is the source of the body's heat: If it isn't snowing, it's windy; if it isn't windy, the body is flooded by language: words run through the mind in a stream. 'Press * at anytime to speak with the front desk,' a voice says, and the desk speaks. The desk speaks. The desk screams.

Desks don't speak, unless . . . The Book of Mormon is the word of God. It joins the Bible as one of the most remarkable texts in the world. When one re-enters, the room is pristine—fresh towels, clean trash bags, soap, and little mints. One always hopes to suck a little mint before falling asleep. This is why one brushes one's teeth: to smell minty fresh.

At night, in bed, one rests one's head; one presses one's legs against sheets; and the sheets are so miserably clean, it's repulsive—the sheets are repulsively clean. And the TV is droning again: a little talking head speaks and, paying no attention, one closes one's eyes, mouth, and lips. The throat expands, contracts in an action known as breathing, and even when the mouth is closed, the throat continues breathing. And this is how a ghost stays alive, already half-dead, in the process of dying: a ghost is alive; its corpse is still breathing. When the corpse ceases breath, the ghost disintegrates—breaks up into parts—presenting several newly polished chapters of the book that will propel the lyric narrative—(its acute language must convey the speaker's mind—her inner heart, gone dead and buried, though never quite at rest). Thus, to disintegrate, the body of the text must henceforth be blind; must unfurl, become ash; become wind, loss of breath.

Human corpses lack organelles, rot beneath the surface, odor of decaying fish. To clone the deceased, dig a pet up from the ground. 'But you'll get into a fight and wind up bloody!' In two days—that is, in one multiplied by two twenty-four hour intervals of time—a narrow, long casket will support Father's cadaver, form a cushion between his half-dead body and the ground. All of the rooms in the morgue are on the same ground—*ground*, from the English verb 'to grind': to reduce to particles or powder by crushing. The truck was grinding slowly up the main road connecting the lake to the center of town. Father was fishing; no doubt, the truck drove up behind him. The lake's ice ruptured. His body sunk with little noise. All sound becomes vapor in snow.

A LOVELY DAY

Last week it snowed each day: ice crystals freezing, white on the lake, which subsided, causing his body to fall. The land fell away in a steep bank; a body falls to the ground before it is pronounced dead. It is not snowing so heavily now.

In summer, 'gone swimming'—out for a swim, Father and . . . 'A lovely day for a swim,' remember him saying, though a person's power to remember is always deformed. 'A lovely day,' remember him saying, and the door of the house is so kindly re-opened; then the door of the house is shut, closed. To re-open it, swivel its knob. But its knob is no longer affixed! It has been placed on the ground, mounted to the ground with permanent adhesive. One would have to take a hammer to the thing, hack away at the thing until the thing breaks, at which point the thing would no longer exist in this space—the present—nor would it exist in the past. To be hammered away from the past, to be blown away from the present, is to exist in a liminal state far away from the door, away from the turning hand and the dull repose of sleep. Oh! One no longer possesses enough strength to sleep, nor should one allow the knob to remain stuck on the ground, where it is beginning to rain, the ground; the ground is raining again: one living species, one dead ecosystem. And the thing created the present, the present ever-imploding—(a peculiar implosion; an implosion nonetheless)—thus the present is ever so drastically stuck, and the hands must cup their palms around the thing, pull the thing until the thing detaches from the ground, giving way to the past.

And thus the past re-opens:

It is not snowing so heavily now, though what is not seen is always meant to break. Human beings are made of ice, crystals that fall through the body, freeze until they melt, discharge, and then detach atop the ice atop the lake. The crystals are frozen. The lake is crystal. A body becomes frozen crystal at the moment of its death. 'Get your carcass out of bed,' remember him saying, 'dead or alive,' remember him saying, and the moment he said it, he died. 'I want to teach you a lesson,' he said in his voice, his male human voice; and no, the lesson was not clear; it was opaque. What scarcely seems sufficient is always opaque: opacity cannot be seen, according to judges. And thus it came to pass that his whole heart was crystal ice. As if it was never affected. As if frozen, self-consciously so. And the lake is so cold, so bright blue. It is the first day of hunting season, and a deer's slaughtered carcass rests across the ground. The scene is bloody, covered in blue blood. The scene is frozen stiff. And blood spreads—pools on the ground—soaking the slaughtered deer's neck, once covered in fur. If the slender arrow missed its half-dead target, the deer would be fur-covered, still. But the arrow did not miss its target; it shot through the air in a line, a low dose, a sentence containing an excess of nouns pressed up against verbs, organs that both comply and act out. Now the deer is half-dead, half-resembling death; it clings to its body, its ghost. In competition with its ghost, its body rests upon its side to stay alive, half-dead in the fetal position. Woe, sibling of the horse, dead deer, branched and bony: your flesh is meat. Bones are ivory. And if it is well with your ghost, it is well with you, deer. The hardness of the hunter's heart is crystal ice, and Father had always been dead, the temperature of snow. His heart was bright blue. His eyes were pitch black. A deer's veins are blue. It is easy to stare, blinded by black. And if all things seen and heard in the world were written in the mind's notebook, a few things would swell: the crescendo of musical notes in the brain, always building up to a grand chorus—'ooh-ooh-ooh,' 'do-re-mi.' The stem's rounded hook, the note's musical pitch: a female deer, a doe. A female dog, a bitch. And to a certain extent—to place truth on the line—Father had always been dead, been stone, been cool to the touch: been a building constructed from the mind's nervous rocks and one thick, plaster cast in the shape of his bones. All bones break apart as they wish, crack in the mind while self-consciousness fades. To place one's finger on a trigger—to turn back the hands of a clock—is to re-open the past: to be and keep in touch, remaining hungry for the other, the body, the Father. 'Show me his body cast, please.' 'How can I say no?' Once in the lobby—the autopsy chamber, the room cooling his body—one presses the keys of a piano; one grazes the flesh on a wrist: one traces the past, fingers a deer, and remembers death, the dog, the bitch.

Oh, how it feels to finger something, to exist in the present at last with one touch, which means so many things. 'Once I felt you, now I hear you,' 'Once I loved you, now I would be amiss to not ascribe the past to my heart, my once-hollow organ denoted by red,' a color, a chestnut, the mind's favorite gift.

Like two parallel rivers, fingers glide across the skin's expanse, preventing the grey death. Fingers glide across each eye, each organ free from light, nerves, and constraint. Shadowing death in one clean, sweeping wave, the eyes flutter shut, see and feel nothing: nobody, nil, squat. And two arms cross over the chest in the shape of an 'X,' the sign of the cross. This keeps the heart from exploding. A bullet shot, 'click click,' thus the gun erupted; there is no need to explain why the body is dead. We live on the dead. We walk on the dead. We breathe the dead, we keep the dead, we scatter the dead's ashes. We bury death with fingers, wake fingers up to death. And thereupon sleeps another kind of death: the death of the hand, limb, or wrist. Later, in bed, we ravel into death, stitch-by-stitch; we ball up in a little skein of yarn, a knot, hair the hand proceeds to braid. 'Hey, hey, hey,' death says, dumbfounded.

* * *

Talk Show Host's lips form words, mouth open wide wielding language all over the shore. A symbol— a wave—curls into an arched form, breaks. A bloom of toxic seawater is called a red tide. To wave goodbye, one moves one's hand to and fro, signaling polite wishes at the end of a conversation. An exchange of spoken ideas is only one instance of communication; one may signal good wishes to bodies both dead and alive. 'A lovely day,' remember him saying, and the chrysanthemums were dead when they appeared. The temperature fell, snow was released, blew freely over the ground; to snow is a season. Snowed in for five nights in the autopsy cooler, Father's cadaver is frozen stiff. And though Talk Show Host says one's mood cannot reflect upon a surface, a water body curls into a symbol of unhappiness, sadness indistinguishable in its appearance from madness or elation. To die at the time of one's death is to appear vertically, standing tall, measuring a specified distance. A physical response to death always involves a distant calculation, as to wave goodbye signals the end of a conversation.

'A lovely day,' remember him, deformed.

II

FRIENDS

Father's cadaver rests horizontally in the autopsy chamber, though it cannot be seen. Mortician explains that after Father's body is embalmed, it will be placed inside a cooler for peepers to see. This way, peepers looking into the casket see a corresponding image of Father's cadaver's earlier person. Brains always store copies of the deceased; trouble is, the detailed image of a person's body after death may inflict mental damage.

Drying hair, damp from a shower, think, 'The morgue is a comfortable place.' Its linens and towels are dry-cleaned. Its desks contain menus, phone books, and a Bible to read. And its corridors are long, although the compass's magnetic strip is always out of order, always spins in circles like a pair of eyes (also out of order). To suffer from the spins, to get dizzy, twirl the body around quickly, in circles, until the eyes re-establish focus on one point in space. Regard a dead deer, a mirror, a face. No. A blotchy black dot, simple and smooth, fills in the eyes' steeple ridge, obliterating all that was seen, felt and lost in the past: a pair of blue eyes, crystal clear and easy in the dark; a bright yellow suitcase, faded by travel and age; and two rings engraved with arched waves.

Saddled with the outcome of the truth, crisis hums in the brain, cannot be extinguished, and a visible suspension of smoke, smoke clouds out, and the eye can feel the present in the brain, which contradicts each ring, each symbol of the past, present and future. Wind, it was nothing. Love, it was only a game. As for crisis, it continues without any clear message: a low humming sound in the brain is heard, has been heard, continues to speak. But no words are perceived. Thus the hum whirrs. The hum whirrs. The hum speaks.

And, all day long, the wind sings: sound persists, carries on, and the wind's electric currents pick up speed, blow through trees. In a gesture of grief, crisis hums through the trees without leaving a trace in the wind. 'Buzz-buzz,' hum the insects. 'Zz-zz,' hum the insects. 'Ss-ss,' hum the cicadas, which hover above grief with wide, open wings, as the low humming sound, devoid of speech, sings.

Drying hair, damp from a shower, notice the floor, walls, and ceiling, all covered in nicotine stains. The floor is misshapen and crooked, and beneath its baroque carpet steer the dirigible ants who dodge death in a swarm, a low flock, a crowded army that infests every narrative regardless of its story, and there are stories of the morgue. One story begins:

Once upon a time, the floor, walls, and ceiling were stained. Once, the morgue was falling apart, and its physical decay induced unease inside a person's brain, her twisted mind. Each day, the morgue fell apart. More and more. Days went by. More and more. Was the morgue in her mind? Even its employees assumed shapes, heavy outlines: physical forms that a person could not ignore—no, she could never ignore the ghostlike tracing of Apparition floating through the morgue; she trembled at the sight. Thought she: 'I too may one day give up the ghost.' Then she picked up the phone.

'Front desk,' a voice says, and the heart, caught by surprise, beats at the sound. A voice, a male human voice, however momentary, sounds in the ear like the voice of a friend, a familiar person one knows. Now the water lily painting looks gorgeous on the wall— fragrant, tall, and bulbous—trumpet-shaped. Outside, it is snowing; the beach is covered in snow: micro-scopic flakes that join together, make white the beach, and ring in the ear like the *crack* of the lake.

'Front desk,' The Voice says, and a voice, a male human voice, speaks. The room appears unpainted, blank. Say, 'Hello.' Say, 'I've noticed nicotine stains,' and notice The Voice's steady breath on the line, a source of inspiration. Say, 'They look easy to clean.' Say, 'I noticed them on the ceiling today.'

Silence ensues, a gap in conversation during which a mass of stars appears, swarms up. Two eyes roll back, stare into the brain, and the brain's frontal lobe turns plum-colored, magenta. Together, the stars all resemble the shape of a face, although the eyes, nose, and mouth are misaligned, out of order. Down the corridor, a sign reads: OUT OF ORDER, and a length of masking tape covers the gumball machine's coin slot. Oh, gumball, gumball no one chews. How, then, must a person eat you?

'I'll send Groundskeeper up,' says The Voice, and his voice, a male human voice, hovers in the brain like an insect with wings, rings out like the sound of a spoon against glass, and there is tension in its silences, as if language sleeps underneath its surface or between each breath. Silence is what the heart needs, requires in order to breathe. Still, a voice, a male human voice, whirrs about the morgue's halls, travels down its endless corridors until it seeps into the baroque carpet which absorbs sound, silence, and speech.

A voice, however speechless, dwells in the morgue and the mind and the brain, insisting a person is never alone—that no, a person, regardless of her solitude, is never alone, and however dumbfounded she may be by grief, a person is always in the company of others, strangers wholly unaware of the circumstances surrounding Father's death; nonetheless, fine company they keep, keep.

'Do you smoke?' The Voice says, and his voice echoes through the telephone's receiver as water in a cavern drips—*drip-drip-drip*, water drips; *drip-drip-drip*, a spigot drips; *drip-drip-drip*, the shower drips. One's hair is now dryer than before.

The mind repeats the question: *Do you smoke?*

Say, 'Why?' Say, 'Do you?' And think—one may experience another person's voice on the phone without feeling distance; one may greet desolation in a crowd of faceless persons; or, one may come face to face with death in the autopsy chamber, and death's casual nudity may leave the body feeling lightheaded, dry in the throat. No one will know.

'I smoke,' The Voice says, and his voice, his male human voice, provides little relief from feeling alone. No one will know. Amidst the darkness, soap, and little mints—once newly replaced, now strewn on the floor—the brain is ablaze, cannot make decisions of sound mind without impulsively reacting to the body's rapid currents, which curl into depression every time emotion breaks.

Say, 'I smoke too.' A lie—the body has excreted a lie in response to The Voice, his voice stuffed with roses, and a peculiar anxiety now overtakes the body, works its way up from the ground toward the mouth's crooked teeth, which are chattering now from the sound of his breath, or is it the cold?

* * *

A few minutes later, meet The Voice. 'Follow me.'

Following The Voice—his voice, a male human voice—down a stairwell, a concrete hallway that reeks, through a door under a sign marked EMERGENCY EXIT, the body falls into a coma, a state of deep indifference marked by a blank look. That which separates one person from another is always marked by a blank look, a distance kept by holding one's arm out at a length, which results in the mind never moving too close. The Voice extends his hand, offers a smoke. His hand is dry, blue, and cracked at the knuckles. And the smoke, white and shaped like a tube, is a poisonous flower, a summary of death taken into the body by a *léger de main*—a lightness of hand—whereupon the brain fills with smoke, the mind fills with smoke, and the lungs fill with smoke until they turn black, unable to take air in, expel out, or blow.

'When was the last time you smoked?' The Voice says.

Think backwards. 'Can't remember.'

A visible suspension of smoke presses between, clouds out. The dead can see the air just like the lungs revile flames without conviction. The Voice reaches out his blue hand, his dry ocean. 'Your hair is dark; the snow makes it light,' he says, as if this statement is a poignant observation that will cause the blank look to dissolve, thereby bridging the gap between deep indifference and friendship. Rest assured, this face-to-face meeting is not about friendship—think, 'no, not at all,' watching his hands tremble blue from the cold. There, in the wind, in the snow, think 'two bodies,' think, 'a little carnal disruption; shut the door,' think, 'in the big picture, the door will re-open,' and then shut the door, still ajar in the brain, open to the possibility that death may be worth keeping, may be worth saving in a book filled with words, white space, and punctuation.

Say, 'Have you ever been in love?' and The Voice—his voice—a male, human voice—says, 'I once fell in love with a woman.'

A fool falls in love. One who dwells in indifference dwells at a distance from love, from its unexpected currents and the lonesome tumbling that causes a person to fall on her knees, if she falls. And there is never any reason to fall, to become so attached to another that one is driven to say, 'I once fell in love,' followed by an ellipsis, '...', a trail leading down a path into—what? Some fatal dream? One grows weak from conflating the future and past, and the ellipsis, '...', always leads into an exposed empty vat, the interior of an urn whose lid has been removed, whose ashes have been spread into water where, in time, everything dissolves, giving way to the past.

Look out at the horizon—the illuminated skyline against the dark and snow—and think, 'The heart is to blame.' Think, 'Indeed, the heart is the source of all blame, and the dead may be to blame for the living's misery.' If only the living could accept the dead's innocence.

Say, 'Who loved who first,' eyeing the clock that glows midnight above the town's lit chamber. And the smoke is but a little stump now; The Voice's hands have stopped shaking, overcome by the cold. Meanwhile, a blank look has dropped down into the heart, and each minute that passes is weighed down by grief: the empty space between the heart, mind, and brain.

'Love wasn't something we discussed,' The Voice says, inhaling.

Say, 'But you had sex?'

'Sex is dull,' The Voice says. 'Do you have friends?'

Say, 'Why?'

'Do you want to be friends?'

Look toward the center of town. It is snowing quite heavily now.

Say, 'Maybe.' Say, 'We'll just have to trust that one of us won't fall in love.'

A fool falls in love, becomes suddenly cold. Then the ocean turns to stone, becomes static. And a heart turns to ice in the autopsy chamber, though no heart controls its own heat.

'I don't think that will be a problem,' The Voice says, lowering his eyes in a contrary signal, a wave meant to disorient any fixed impression of the heart in the mind. Eyes, which sob and have sobbed and have taken the place of their sobbing, have already entered into a relationship with the cylindrical containers of tears that pour out from every high object: the clouds, superimposed in the sky; the showerhead, infinitely circular and impossible to adjust; and the chamber's brightly lit clock, which sounds *tick-tock, tick-tock* every hour, the brain's newfound addiction. Meanwhile, temptation sounds all the time, although the mind, separate from the body, sleeps alone. And The Voice's hands are chafed, so blue and grotesque. Who in the night in the world would ever hold them? His knuckles are tinged with dried blood. His fingernails, jagged and bitten. 'Can I ask you a question,' he says, at which point his hands, his representation of loss, ricochet against the heart's empty space.

A Question

'Can I ask you a question,' The Voice repeats, running his hand along the heart's empty space, which is now full of waves, feelings which flood the heart, make liquid the heart, and take up space. Must crisis enter the heart? Or might the heart open its gates, spill open its contents and reveal itself as wholly self-contained, split apart by death, the stray dog who can scarcely stand to listen to the unexpected waves' dull reverberations—'ooh-ooh-ooh,' *tick-tick-tick*, 'do-re-mi,' etcetera, and so on and so on, ad infinitum. Think, 'How incessant,' etcetera, and so on and so on, ad infinitum, and run one finger along the split heart's grooves; drift along inside its little chambers toward The Voice's lonely hands, now cut off at the wrists.

Turn toward The Voice; meet his gaze. Say, 'Ask me a question.' Examine his face. His nose is crooked. His eyes are black. He breathes, and his forehead takes deep breaths. His lips are moving. His lips are a trap. Think, 'He is, to be sure, odd-looking.' Think, 'Does he know how odd-looking he is?'

The Voice lowers his gaze. 'Do you think'—beat—
'as they say'—beat—'that love is a state of existence?'

Repeat the expression: *Love is a state of existence.*
Knot the mind around its nouns and swallow whole
its minor parts until the body experiences a new type
of death, the death of a sentence. Think, 'Love is a type
of existence,' and the expression dwells in the brain;
but one knows—has always known—that love's origins are, to be sure, in a relationship with death. This
dispute between abstractions will never be resolved;
and, once again, snow falls in bright white sheets
along the surface of the mind's protective enclosure.
Love is a greeting, a death.

Once again, the autopsy chamber creeps into mind:
a bright room, devoid of windows, that, regardless of
season, glows in the night. Indeed, fluorescent lights
are always flickering, establishing their brightness in
the night, and they bequeath upon the chamber a pure
and simple madness: perfume mixed with Father's
dead body's unfortunate scent. Think, 'Formaldehyde
scent,' and each syllable takes up space in the brain,
which is now covered with a mask to shield the heart,
which should have never been born; no, the heart
must never give birth to itself. Father's body is frozen
stiff; no formaldehyde could do the trick: his body
required treatment beyond a normal case. And his
frozen corpse absorbs the light, which shines from

the ceiling, making white his skin, his skin white like the snow which covered the ice atop the lake. And The Voice is now narrowing his eyes; he is twisting his hands. He is accenting his words with his hands—his ugly, disembodied hands tinged with dry blood, his fingernails jagged and bitten. Think, 'How disgusting.' Think, 'What a shame.' Who in the world in the night will ever hold him?

Say, 'Love is a little like death.' Say, 'I don't know what to think.' And perhaps this view has never been enunciated quite in this way; perhaps now the story's dénouement has become too easy, and now is the time to uncross his hands—unravel his hands—hold steady his hands in order to feel his hands against the heart's unsteady beat. Say, 'What do you think,' once again eyeing the clock that glows above the lit chamber.

'Love is a question of perspective,' says The Voice, and although the sentence enters the mind, its language becomes muddled. 'Also, love is absurd.' What does he mean? Does he mean what he says? Soon, The Voice—his voice—a male, human voice—becomes lost in the head.

A fool falls in love, loses purpose. And he who cannot bear to fall in love? His response is left to the judges. Nasty death is left to cool inside a box, and the autopsy chamber—the heart—is so full of itself, one cannot motion to free it. To free the heart from itself—from the body's emotional death—reveals another kind of death: the death of the lungs, which expel language, deep breath.

The Voice is now folding his hands at his chest in a solemn gesture, as if inspiring some visual connection between his hands and his heart will change the body's influence upon the mind. 'No,' the body says. Although, yes—of course, indeed—The Voice is kind, holding his hands over the heart, inducing a new and unexpected feeling. But his aversion to death—the trust he places in life; his fixation upon love and lust and physical force, and his need to cause the heart distress . . . No, the heart must never accept this. The heart must wholly reject his physical presence and refocus its lens upon shock: the image of Father's body cascading through ice; the burden of Father's body in the autopsy chamber, preserved in the ice; and color, which causes the world to take on the illusion of possessing physical form, form independent from water, 'blue blue,' although water pools at the foot of his chest, in the palm of his heart. And thus, in light of his physical presence, should one refuse the cold— say, offer The Voice a glass? Groundskeeper seems to think so, guarding the morgue on her knees, her ivory bones curling up toward her mouth, her little smiling mouth revealing a secret in the shape of—what is it? An upside-down moon?

Say, 'I feel thirsty,' eyeing the clock, the snow and water on the ground, Groundskeeper on her knees, and The Voice's ugly hands—such dry, blue, and awful hands—and refocus the brain on hunger before the heart devours the mind. Now the mouth closes, refusing to utter new sound. Sound fades into a yawn, a yawn fades into sleep, and, when the body wakes, it will wake alone: only the sound of a phone will echo the heat of his voice—The Voice—a male, human voice—for which the brain once felt love, now discontent. Because to love during a time of grief—to re-open the heart, to bloom open the heart's dead bouquet—is to admit that grief is not the end; that grief—regardless of its heavy weight atop the mind, brain, and shoulders—is never the end. But, alas, the mind is certain. Grief is, at this moment, the end. Otherwise, the heart would, within moments, re-open: re-open to grass, sleep, and The Voice's uncanny physical form, which embodies all angles, reflecting the essence of color. However, in the present, one is left to deal with grief's fragile repercussions, which are at once unwelcome and embraced. So the question is not: How does one make do the heart? The question is: How does the heart make its own grave?

ATRIUM

A loop is a path leading around the morgue, though it is never circular. One begins by descending stairs, flat platforms arranged in a series. The staircase ascends; the staircase descends. Charting a map of the loop, the word 'circumambulation' drifts into mind.

Stairwells are white, the color of milk, opaque and secluded, always. Note the painted concrete walls below the cylindrical pipes. Note the pipes are beige, a shade of brown, suntanned and of unknown origin. Notice the total absence of sound: It fades, grows faint, then . . .

Singer is singing. One exits the stairwell and enters the lobby, a glass-covered, moonlit atrium. WELCOME, a sign says, PLEASE SIGN-IN IN PERSON. 'Person,' from the Old French *persone*, is derived from the Latin *persona*. Wearing a mask cast in wax, plaster, or clay, an actor assumes a persona, a character, a likeness of a person's pattern of behavior.

The morgue elongates, its walls stretch out, and a phonograph plays. 'I can't help lovin' that man,' a phonograph plays, and Singer is singing. Singer's cadaver is icy, pale blue. Her blood is alkaline fluid. And she must have blue in her blood, must paint her blood with the cold: a dark color not not in use, not of a sound mind. Father's death was unexpected; it happened unexpectedly. And all that one feels, one must feel in the dark: the cold, saltwater heart cannot sing its own blues, cannot confront itself in the dark, nor admit 'yes' to the truth. 'No,' says the heart to the truth. 'The deer was alive.' But the deer—the poor, lean-necked deer—was shot dead at the scene, and the trees too were dead, the town dead, the phone dead, the brain dead, silence dead, and yes, the heart admits, Father is dead too. He has been dead for days. And to place truth into words—to string the truth on a line, a low dose, a long sentence—his body will never return, will never again come alive. What's a person to do? What must one's heart retain? Once the sun sets, the heart sets down a record, presses 'play.'

Singer's voice is very much unlike The Voice—his voice—a male human voice that one hears in the mind, reminding the heart to stay open. 'Even the drone of TV is a sound,' The Voice says: 'Choose to listen.' Thus the heart—the saltwater heart—pays attention, listens closely, but the drone—zz-zz-zz, *buzz-buzz-buzz*, etcetera and so on and so on, ad infinitum—reveals nothing.

63

One may perceive Singer's cadaver's pale blue skin, but one cannot touch. To touch—to extend fingers, to run fingers along a windowsill, parapet, or sink—is to enclose some handy stimulus, to close one hand around the heart and whisper 'shh,' which settles nothing. Alas, the heart is weak with lamentation. In the hotel, alone in its bed—devoid of blood, weight and emotion—it sleeps. But it keeps thumping— *thump-thump-thump*, *tap-tap-tap*—and these beats always add up to grand applause, which, collectively ringing, repulses the brain, whose erstwhile deeds may also be dark, unforeseen. Heart pleads with the brain, nonetheless: 'perceive, perceive.' 'Please take me with you,' it beckons to see. So should one admit defeat, give in to the deed, or deny the request to submit? On rare occasions, heart calms. Sometimes, it gives in to touch. Alone in sleep, it continues to grieve, hardwired to the brain's awareness: consciousness.

Singer is singing, recalling a song from years ago below the balcony. 'I can't help lovin' that man,' Singer sings, and persons listen, attuned to sound, vibrations that drift through the morgue into space. Alas, life cannot grasp death, cannot grip the dead with two hands; nor shall the constellations formed by Singer's voice be broken apart by the dead, the dead, the dead—oh! Singer links the living score back to the half-dead composer.

'I can't help lovin' that man,' Singer sings, and emotion grips the score, pleads with the dead to return to the glass-covered, moonlit atrium. 'Fish got to swim, birds got to fly, I got to love one man 'til I die,' Singer sings, and the phonograph rings out—its sound is crystal clear—the phonograph rings out; thus the audience drifts through a half-dead song whilst looking at the moon: a crystal chandelier that illuminates even the dead's reflection.

In the glass-covered lobby—the autopsy room, the room driven to death by his body—water lilies hang majestically from half-dead canvases, weep themselves a succession of notes: small, handwritten reminders that grief will pass like a ghost, and life will continue despite the body's termination. Apparition dwells in the morgue day-by-day, haunting those who measure their lives via a string of deaths. First, a deer died. Then Father died. Now, Singer is singing, and persons dressed in penguin suits listen to her song—'I can't help lovin' that man,'—they listen to her song and encircle the room, drinking whiskey, champagne, and Very Special Brandy. Three persons wearing pantsuits look the same, eating around a table piled with lox, smoked fish the morgue serves before dinner.

Singer's mask is singing, and no one, including Singer, can picture the mask. No one sees. In French,

'Il n'y a personne ici,' where 'personne' refers to no one. No one perceives Singer's mask as persons loop around the morgue, humming. No one ascends the stairwell in reverse descent, fingertips tracing the balcony. No one looks down from the balcony; no one sees Singer's long black leather gloves. No one sees Singer, hears Singer singing. And thus Singer's mask implies a face, a connotation made explicit by the presence of amnesia, which causes persons to forget exactly whom Singer recalls.

And a person stands in a corner, dressed for an absence. As the soirée proceeds into night, a person's brain rings out a fever pitch: 'Bravo for Singer! Bravo for Singer's long black leather gloves!' Like a glove, night is black; it gives Singer a round of applause. 'How reprehensible,' the brain thinks, and every time the revolving door loops back, it is difficult to not take this thought to task, to heart, to the pantry, where, in the middle of the night, he would retreat for a snack: dry cereal, always—cold milk makes it difficult to sleep. And the weight of this thought causes the brain to weep; and now Singer is singing a new song, an elegy for long-departed love.

'Blues on my mind, blues all around my head,' Singer sings. 'I dreamed last night that the man that I love was dead.'

'I went to the graveyard, fell down on my knees. I wrung my hands, and I wanted to scream, but when I woke up, I found it was only a dream.'

Repeat the lyric: *When I woke up, I found it was only a dream.* 'If only,' the brain thinks. 'If only death was a dream.' Together, the soirée goers applaud 'bravo, bravo'—their own heated, fever pitch—although to hear the crowd applauding is to hear the crowd in mourning. As in Quaker mass, one must feel inspired to stand, to speak, grieve, to applaud each silence until silence is no longer pronounced, until a song exists in the air 'in memoriam,' in memory of the deceased. R.I.P.

Aboveground, trees cover the deceased and provide shade—a dark area apart from the sun—which encloses all funeral-goers. Underground, dirt is thick and sturdy. And Father, dear Father, 'your memory causes my heart to fall out,' to splatter flat on the ground until all is left behind, until the hollow body begins to trace out its shell-like regions: the ribcage, chest, and pelvic girdle grieve until the bones are rearranged, resemble a skeleton, a museum exhibit, a body shell case. In case the glass shatters, document the past with exquisite repose; reconfigure bones until they order the mind without disrupting the brain, which is constantly at work to put the pieces back in order. Say to the brain: 'Replenish the images you refuse to keep; refuse stasis. Resign from eating away at the thing; eat the thing. Remember all that is needed to lead a most pleasurable life'—food, water, and sex—all urgent things. But nothing is as urgent as the ambulance's siren, which echoes from afar and is heard in the distance. And a person dressed in black always blends into her absence, although her expression is soured by grief, shoved into the ground, hung upside-down from a tree until the gravedigger throws up. When a person throws up, she is emptied. When a match is blown out, light is extinguished. Again, in a minor key—what a terrible mess: one throws up. One throws up. One throws up.

Soon, one begins eating again, and although one feels the opportunity to lie awake, to think, eat, and be consumed by the turbulent waves that crash into the mind, body, and brain, one thinks, 'Something is missing,' and Singer's pendulum sways, a slender form. And the elegant soirée goers imbibe and laugh; the evening is tepid and, to reassemble the puzzle, to piece together the pieces until the missing puzzle piece appears—why should a person assume a detective persona? Truth is, a person is always eating, never thinking, and this lack of thinking causes the entire brain to feel consumed. Even while lying down, one feels consumed. And this consumption is hence known as absence: the lack of forgetting, of constantly remembering the missing person, place, or thing.

A Common Resemblance

Hotel is a noun, an established block of speech. Block—a singular noun—is also a verb, wood from the trunk of a tree. A tree is any body severed from its limbs. The cut down limbs of trees are also known as log cabins. A log cabin is a house; it is also a hotel. Inside, human bodies dwell, think at length about disease.

A hotel may look like a house. This is a common resemblance. Persons dwell inside a hotel—think, 'Dwell,' regarding death. Think, 'Persons die,' and 'Persons live'; engrave the fact of life and death on persons. Still-grieving persons dwell in the mind, superimpose faces over living persons' heads. A face is what distinguishes one person from the next: The eyes, nose, and mouth align in descending order, or they do not. When a person sees an unknown face approach, her ability to distinguish is lost. When one person loses a face, she experiences amnesia. There are two kinds of amnesia: full-memory, in which a person loses everything, and prosopagnosia, the inability to recognize a face.

Hotel rooms contain mirrors, reflective surfaces upon which persons' faces are reflected, or they are not. Below a mirror is a sink—a basin whose water supply is drained, deprived of energy. Rooms in hotels empty; a garbage can is emptied; a water glass is empty of its contents when it is set at the foot of the bed. To pour remaining liquid out, one tilts the glass over the sink in a downward sloping position. Liquid floods the drainpipes in a constant stream.

'Damn those clogged pipes,' Groundkeeper says, kneeling next to her bright yellow bucket. And the heart clogs; the sound of a foot clogs. In light of his death, Four Men roam the halls, and Father's body is cold—colder each day—and emits death in the hallway, in every corner of the morgue. Tomorrow, he will be no longer. He will no longer be cold.

Said Groundskeeper: 'Damn those clogged pipes,' looking straight into the front layer of the eye, referred to with one word—'cornea'—beautiful, in fact, despite its formlessness. One word—'cornea'—travels through the mind, brain, and body; it rests in the palm of a hand like a coin in a slot, and a lever sets the word in motion: *cornea*. The word takes hold of the mind with its clarion call, and the mouth utters a phrase—*transparent formlessness*—and now the room is perceived with two eyes, with one half-dead, empty gaze. And while the hands feel the room with two palms, the word—'cornea'—carries on in the brain.

Groundskeeper carries a bright yellow bucket, wipes the floor on her knees. The bucket rests on the floor, and Father's cadaver will soon no longer be at rest in the morgue, the blue around his eyes so crystal-clear and fine. And Groundskeeper's eyes look concerned: 'Look away,' she says, eyeing his body, his expressionless gaze in the light. Say to Groundskeeper: 'No, I was there when he died,' and a wave of shock cascades through the brain like a wave.

Presumably, something in this scene must evoke color, but must it be the bright yellow bucket or Groundskeeper's gnarled, gray hair? 'No,' the brain thinks. The body must reject external forms and refocus the mind: visualize a voice, say, or the absence of physical form, a disembodied wave that strikes each time the mind remembers he was once there—atop the lake, then submerged under ice. In the course of a moment, his life ran its course. He died. And all that remains in this moment is unfocused contempt for the dead: The light is too fluorescent, impersonal, and cold. Think, 'dumb bitch,' turning to Groundskeeper—the mind turning, once again, to death.

'Are you okay?' Groundskeeper says, eyeing the body up and down. Her eyes traverse the body down and up and down, and she is relentless in her pursuit. 'Are you okay?' she repeats and, in this instance, her repetition reverberates. *Are you okay*, demands the mind. *Are you okay*, echoes the brain. 'Dumb bitch,' says the heart, and the image of a dog appears foggy at first, then it grows. Then it fades. Fades out.

No longer a preposition, refuse fades out into the past: a space the present moment cannot dwell in without grief. To stand in pieces at the center of the present—to spread the body out into an 'X' so one's hands and feet press against grief's equidistant corners—is to be shoved into burying streams, streams that drown out drainpipes as the hands and feet deform. In turn, the eyes, nose, and mouth all take on grotesque features: the eyes become sallow and jaundiced, the nose caked in salt. And from its hollow O, the mouth emits dead leaves: O, the mind demands that each dead leaf peels off its sheets, one layer at a time.

A sudden death. A frozen death. A random, forgotten death. A china, glass, or hard cash death. A death that demands grief, demands little grief. And as one reviews the will, it will appear there is so much upon which the deceased rests. 'O,' the mind exhales. 'What a terrible mess.'

A clump of hair is nestled in the sink. Whose hair is it? Apparition drifts through the chamber with rounded lips. 'Ooh, ooh, ooh,' his mouth emits, or is it an owl? Surely the room is private, and it is impossible to tell the owl from the ghost: Both are perched on the limb of a tree, which is already dead, knocked down. A document says so. A document says: 'I, [Full Name of Person Making the Will], a resident of [City, State], hereby make this Will. I was born on [Date of Birth] in [Place of Birth—City, State]. I will my property to the following persons.'

'I have one living child' reads the will, and outside it rains—rains and rains and rains—and refuse floods the drainpipes, streams and pours away—a preposition—into nonexistence, the space between death (the stray bitch) and two palms, not to mention the past. 'I have one living child,' reads the will, and where there is one, there may also be two: two hands, two fists, two of each finger. Each finger grows out from each hand; each finger is autonomous—acts independently—and makes the decision to point down—a preposition—toward the baroque carpet. Fingers work in tandem as the body works: as a machine, an apparatus that depends upon its own power to function. Missing power, the hands are unable to function. And thus two hands function together delicately, as lattices: wooden strips that work together, interlace.

EGGS IN BED

Breakfast is served while it's still dark outside. Batter pours into an iron.

A painting on the dining room wall depicts a water lily spread open across a pad of circular leaves. The painting, a stock reproduction, evokes the morgue's secluded garden, a place to stop and think and gaze upon the ground, perplexed by a common resemblance. 'You look like him,' a person said, referring to the *face*, from the Latin *facies*, meaning 'form': the outward shape a structure, word, or sentence takes.

One is 'sentenced to death.' Choked by a necklace of language, it is this expression—'sentenced to death'—that echoes in the brain, luminescent as the moment is dark, as the the sky is white and thick as milk, and it seems unreal—the sky is white and thick as milk, and a necklace of language is choking a person to death—sentencing someone to death—and each word knocks against the brain like a brick to the head, uninterrupted—each word knocks against the brain like a brick to the head, and the mind's argument is this: one is sentenced to death, the dog, the bitch.

The sentence speaks. Says the sentence: 'Grief is a garden, a painting depicting lilies, goldfish and . . .' Goldfish are orange; lilies are pink; plants are bright green. Does color affect what is seen, what takes place outside? Painting is water. Water, a lily. 'You'll be left with egg on your face,' remember him saying, and the eggs begin to taste chalky. The mouth has the ability to remember, but not the brain. Thinking of food, one almost always feels disgusted. Interrupted by an ellipsis, '...', one thinks of nothing at all or fills in the blank. Has anything happened at all?

Repeat the question: *Has anything happened at all?* Gaze into dark as morning becomes light. Soon the funeral-goers will proceed into the dining room, pile their plates high with waffles, bacon, and eggs. And they will look mournful in black; they will refrain from eye contact unless to say they're sorry—'so sorry' and 'thinking of you during this difficult time.'

Has anything happened at all? To answer the question, one must first empty the mind of its contents and think back to the very first day. 'To avoid grief,' Groundskeeper said, 'Float along the swimming bath's edge.' And still the body floats through grief. The morgue's physical form fades away, and it's true—the throat is the part of the body containing pet fish: limbless, cold-blooded creatures that live underwater, rise to the ceiling after death. Some fish disobey logic and sink, but fish never drown. Submerged in the throat's floodwater, wildflowers, fallen trees, and colored weather, fish must be dead, must be the temperature of snow—of light white, frozen fish; colorless fish; cold-hearted fish; fish without bones—is it truly a fish? Formless fish; late pet fish; overanxious, ugly fish that are easy on the heart although the heart is frozen stiff, and there are no bones—can it truly be a fish? How can a fish without bones, without scales, without fins, without gills—(loss of breath)—without skin, lungs, or two-chambered hearts or a bowl, tank, or dome— how can a fictitious fish see through the glass?

Dead fish are at rest in the morgue, and the throat, lips, and flesh of two palms are upturned toward the ceiling, covered in nicotine stains. Here and there, the body floats in vain to understand his death, but all that remains in the brain is an image: the crystal lake upon which color reflects, where light spreads freely through the mind as ice expands across the lake— light spreads through the brain as redwoods stretch across the mind, thus one narrow strip of the brain is covered in growth, trees, and shrubbery. Sand, salt, and wind spray through fog, and one species must remain forever colorless.

Water and fish form one kind of support: one strange, therapeutic relief in light of death, the brain's dawn. 'Float along the swimming bath's edge,' Groundskeeper said, and only in water did clarity come, taking on the shape of questions in the mind. *What happened?* the mind demands. *Has anything happened at all?* These questions repeat in the mind as star patterns form in the sky, rearranging the stars in the mind.

From the moment one checked into the morgue, the mind was filled with stars. Some were wandering, some properly fixed, and others took on the shape of an asterisk—*—and some were used to rate the morgue, to indicate its service. Two were glowing steady with no flame; two possessed a heightened color that caused the face to turn green. The face turned green; the lips turned green; and the throat, eyes and cheeks all turned green with disgust. And the path to the beach is circuitous: It involves tracing a map from the morgue to the woods, tracing a path from the woods to the beach. It involves lines, lines correspond to each place, and each destination along the path is denoted by an asterisk, a *, a little thing resembling a star in its shape.

In the morgue, persons die of disgust. Such a state-ment may be regarded as callous, yet the moment persons touch another or the dead, death is aroused, and arousal and loss are linked. A callus is formed. 'Front desk,' The Voice said, and his hand slid across the mind in a flatline. 'Here you are,' said the thing, the star, and the beach opened. Grief opened. An ultimatum was given: death or a chestnut? But a chestnut is impossible to crack! It is a wholly unmanageable task, a nut to crack, to deconstruct its shell so the fruit is exposed, made visible by the act of uncovering.

At the edge of death, a person holds another's hand between two sheets, bedclothes draped over bodies to trace ghosts. A ghost, distinct from a body, exemplifies paleness, and all the lines are intact, lilies perfectly rendered, so pink and detailed in the light. Do Not Carry Buffet Plates Away from the Dining Area, a sign says, and light shines: A door is unlocked. 'Here you are,' says the star, and the room is pristine, free of shrubbery. And as this will is written with the intent of reuniting the dead with the living, the mind now turns to ghosts. Ghosts are hidden; the will is unwritten. Sleeping alone in a bed, one almost always feels a hand: a presence felt, cool to the touch, under one's clothes. Still in the autopsy chamber, dead Father is asleep, thus to withstand the night alone—to stand in pieces at the foot of death—a person must think, 'I'm going to die,' and grip the hand, take a breath. But the hand refuses to hold back, and a person fails to feel aroused, and grief takes hold, nags on all night. Death presses from the other side.

The First Night

Take a moment to imagine depression's thrust on speech. Think, 'written words,' think, 'signs,' think, 'ceaseless punctuation.' Think, 'metaphors,' think, 'morgue,' think, 'more than one solution,' think, 'cosine spiraling out'—a preposition—into a never-ending cycle, a black hole. And now open the mouth; utter a sound. The sound's reverberations fade into the air. Sound may also fade into another person's ear. Like color, sound requires concentration—although it is impossible to concentrate while listening.

Atop Father's grave rests a bouquet of roses, which are making the sign of the cross. 'Bless us, Father,' they pray, making the sign of the cross. 'We have sinned. It has been two weeks since our last confession,' and their eyes, more drunk than before, settle upon the priest, who crosses his arms, legs, and heart. Hoping to die, he crosses his heart. For their sins, he begs forgiveness. 'Forget and forgive what they did,' he prays. 'Amen.'

Repeat the expression: *Amen*. Now all eyes in the mind turn toward the brain, which stores a copy of his image, the deceased. 'A lovely day for a swim,' echoes the deceased, and a voice—The Voice—his male, human voice, floats along the swimming bath's edge; the feeling brain drifts in and out of light, and the body is blue, bluer than before: Color takes possession, brings out physical form.

A morgue is an obtrusive building where the roof and walls are thinking, where the brain and mind drift out to sea on a bateau, yawl, or origami boat. 'Float along the swimming bath's edge,' Groundskeeper said, and Father's half-dead body is the only solid thing in the morgue, the one physical form still at rest in the lobby—in the autopsy chamber, the room cooling his body—and thus the only thing to hold a frame to death.

But what is the frame? How does one frame death? To write down death, to transcribe the mind, provides an account of the thing—his death—and when the present becomes past, it may shed light on the twofold nature of the world—the hotel and the morgue—the structures that support his deceased body, which will soon plummet into the ground, fall through the earth at a speed that mirrors the speed of a lift, a pulley and its weight. What, you may ask, is the lesson of death?

Enclosed in the morgue, one confronts Father's body's death. 'I'm going to teach you a lesson,' his dead mouth says, and the lesson it pronounces makes little to no sense:

'What is death but a reprieve? Each day, the living live in vain, and although one's mind may possess good intentions, one always cracks another's heart, or one's own.

'A sound mirrors the cracking lake before one's death: a hard and insensitive sound that echoes in the mind, over and over until there is no sound left of which to speak, or until the sound echoes through the morgue's secluded halls—echoes in the brain and taps against the brain's four walls with utmost insistence—*tap-tap-tap, tap-tap-tap, tap-tap-tap*. Thus ensues the day. One folds newspaper into one's coat and, hoping to die, boards the train. Seen from the platform, the train fades away. 'How quaint,' one thinks, watching it pull from the station into unconsciousness. And the platform empties; the hotel bar is empty; the morgue's liquor cabinet is emptied of its contents before a person drinks her grief. Be that as it may, the living drink in vain.'

'No,' a person thinks, 'My grief is not in vain.' And thus the heart begins to beat in a steady pattern, a rhythm unknown to the brain, and the brain must poke holes in its dreadful noise, its awful sound, its even tempo which suggests despair, the most featureless grief. *Dumb bitch*, hums the brain in response to the heart. *Dumb bitch*, sings the mind to the brain. And it is remarkable how the connection between the brain, heart and mind causes the body confusion. In order to renounce itself, the body must retreat into itself and turn to formlessness: pain less, detach, and make do—dissolve into wind, loss of breath.

Father's dead mouth shuts. A bottle uncorks. Now it is time to play dead. But before proceeding into death, into the body's swinging rage, one must first unscrew the body's cork, unscrew the ugly worm until it can be unscrewed no more—or until it is strangled, choked. If, on the other hand, one must treat the body as one treats a glass of wine, then the body must undergo a little aeration—must not be sipped until air has been introduced—and, once more, his body must be siphoned out atop the table. Once more, the throat chokes at the sight.

It is impossible to shut out the unsightliness of his body's degradation on the table where, under fluorescent lights, he is examined before burial. 'Can you identify this body as your Father,' Mortician says. 'Take your time,' Mortician says—and the train pulls back into the station; it had been gone for some time. Outside, sun flickers in atypical fashion: It fully illuminates, is fully alive. And inside, his body's hairs look dark, dead under fluorescent lights. His body is a slaughtered deer, a slab of venison. Sun illuminates the leaves; grass and pollen enter the nose, making it harder to breathe. Air asphyxiates, and his body on the table is his shadow, his dark gloom. And now the sun takes on the shape of the moon, a crescent, and his body rests inside its gentle curvature. At rest atop the moon, he is fishing, no doubt: The moon drifted up behind him as the train drifts back into the station, and wine is red, the worm invasive. And his body is a cork, a plug that kept life in until his death. Now his body rests atop a table, dead. Think, 'Father! Open your eyes. Open your pool of grief, blue below the bark of shut eyelids. Pull the train into the station; fold the newspaper; cross your heart and never die.' But death is massive—explosive—and the eyes, mind, and brain perceive its weight, and the water below the ice atop the lake is cold and blank. Meanwhile, the autopsy results flesh out the circumstance—'asphyxiation,' the paper says: a condition in which air in the lungs is replaced by water. What good would it have done, to survey the ice, deer, or bridge? Planks always held the bridge together, and the deer was already dead, had been a living dead target forever and ever. And to fish upon a frozen lake, one must first climb upon it, which is exactly what he did.

Dear Father Fish: The entirety of the lake is death. And a gift is a pleasant bequest. Even during periods of grief, a gift is a pleasant bequest. And so a person might mutter, 'Okay, I accept this.' But to accept death's punctuation—that the larynx threatens life—one must never mutter 'okay'; one must always pronounce speech. And one must always refuse to asphyxiate the body, refrain from strangling the neck until its cork pops off. No, the bequest must be spent on an alcoholic beverage—wine—a gift of deep red liquid made from grapes. The grapes are large; the wine, fermented. After four glasses, a person feels nauseous, jetlagged, and uncomfortably cold. 'How quaint,' remember thinking, stumbling into a closet, frozen from the sorrow and the cold. 'This is how it feels to freeze to death.'

A Moment of Silence

To lock oneself away in a dark room far from the sweeping expanse of the city. To grow dark. To explain that what has grown dark is not light, to light the room: The room itself, accompanied by a series of rooms in the brain, is full of stairs—images that swim back and forth between the frontal cortex and the cerebellum, where the brain caves into grief with one cold, clammy palm. No longer. One is unable to write the brain, the skin. Skin, translucent blue film that covers the body, conforms to the body's every curve. So long, dear body. The spine's newly rigid vertical form signals the dead body, lying horribly straight on a desk like a pen, pencil, or marker.

Like a pen, pencil, or marker. The body uncaps itself and glides across a series of blank papers to form a sequence of words, a phrase—'a moment of silence, dead fish—' the body writes, 'dead fish floating in space.' Dead fish float, the crux of his death. In this book, on this beach, dead fish wash up—his body washes up—not as a symbol of death but of slippage: the distance between the parts of a sentence and how these parts are reached.

Descent. The word rings out in the mind, a clarion call. Sweet descent, coated in shellac, *laque en écailles*, is dead, dead fish. And the body is built to inhabit this liminal space, as if slippage exists in a visceral form to appease the living, dead Father. Sometimes a collection of bodies overturns the beach, and the mouth drops open in the shape of an 'O,' but no sound slips out. There are too many bodies; no sound slips out. There are too many dead fish; their fins glide out. They are gone. R.I.P. Fin. And thus there too is the presence of death underground, underwater: the ground's moss-coated deathbed of roses. Roses, roses: 'blue blue,' yellow, or red. 'Let us begin with a moment,' The Priest says, and the roses are silent film grain. Lower the coffin, cover the grave.

Burial

A graveyard is a burial ground, a lawn beside a mausoleum lined with stained glass windows. Stained glass reflects the iris staring straight—completely white—and thus inverts the kind of light that corresponds with seeing; so to speak—to open one's mouth and utter a sound—is to form an intermittent lake around the eye, which tends toward blindsight: an injury that causes a blind eye to see. Inside the casket is blue velvet; however, no one sees. To see, open the casket: Look into the casket and allow access, passage, or a view into an empty space called a shape, a form, a guise which gives rise to something once abstract.

Light is a motionless stone. If you look beneath its gaze, your eye will yield to, play up its luminescence, and the wind will dissolve into contours, the nucleus of death. Thus the sweat begins. But it is not panic nor fright, neither the low sky nor the morning's temperature that commands rise to spring, to consciousness. Nor is it a seasonal fever, a neutral degree of warmth that turns a body into a hot spell the body expires, breathes out. Light, the totality of form, must be discharged, must be sent forth. And now the air is impure, contains an entire body's worth of the most abundant chemical—oxygen—and only trees chopped into bits may suspend its uninterrupted flood. Only nature is so lonely to quarantine a casket underground, to make it function as a tree's roots. A casket is sturdy; a tree's roots are robust. A body must rot in a casket, 'rot rot.' Henceforth trees are no longer the loneliest element: They absorb dried bone, hot coals, cremains. What is sent forth into wind is residual: Ash scatters across rooftops; the deadness of leaves is exposed. If this disenchants the living, let the living be. If a doorway appears, let it be a wooden thing on a hinge with a knob, a body suspended in space. Let headstones rise aboveground and stand tall, vertically, in order to convey a dead cadaver's slot, a deer's footprint in mud. Distance elongated by a freight train's blow departs the station, and a deer comes to life: The winter subsides. And whereupon the graveyard does the group of funeral-goers stand? Around a plot of Astroturf, of course: an artificial grass contained by ribbons marked RESERVED. One funeral-goer smiles: That had been kept in, kept.

That had been kept in, kept, just as the body is kept in, kept: placed inside a casket to be lowered underground with the thing, the burial mechanism. Open the ground. And persons dressed in black clothing, weighted down by absence, stand still and do nothing, fully inert. And their monochromatism is cordial, although black is not a color. One funeral goer spreads open her mouth in a wide 'O,' and 'O,' the casket is closed; its weight plummets into the ground. 'O,' the mouth gapes, and the burial mechanism's lowering straps apply tension to the casket. Discomfort spreads aboveground for funeral goers to perceive, to discern visually with eyes, which are open, blindsighted. And when the lowering straps are detached, tension is released: The funeral goers abandon their gaze; the casket descends. To descend is a motion: Funeral-goers feel action, the force of the casket descending into the ground. Ground is mud; grass is ground. Pressed down by the weight of bystanders, the ground sinks further and further into the earth. But, 'O,' the mouth gapes, the earth is pitiless under its own weight. It sinks into itself, devours itself and reproduces itself as a perennial crop or compost heap. With two eyes, the ground sees, but no pair of eyes can see into the casket: Under the weight of inertia, neither the earth nor the funeral goers see. They only gaze into distance, into fog that so consumes a life with invitations: You are invited, hope you can make it, R.S.V.P., *s'il te plait; je t'adore*, R.I.P.

Plummeting into nothingness, the casket sinks: A spring is released; gears rotate outward in a counterclockwise motion. One funeral goer falls onto her knees, falls into blindsight and chokes up a necklace. Woe, now a necklace is choked: A person is sentenced to death. And the fog is so dense, so cold, 'I cannot stand its thickness,' she moans, and fog encloses the graveyard that encloses the deceased. And a spring is released, gears rotate out. What is the lesson? Must a lesson be learned? Has anything happened at all? When the lowering straps are detached, tension will set sadness free: To descend, a motion. The casket will descend into the ground, where it will rest, sleep in darkness, and the living will continue gathering losses, focusing the mind on fixed points: stars, fish, or flowers that symbolize the deceased. What happened? Has anything physical form? Under its own weight, the casket sinks at a controlled speed. Weighted down by a second body, the burial mechanism fails.

ACKNOWLEDGEMENTS

Grateful acknowledgement to the editors of *LIT* and The Organism for Poetic Research's *PELT* for publishing 'Friends' and 'Check-In' from *Burial*, respectively. 50 words from 'A Lovely Day' were published in *[C.]*, Mud Luscious Press's Stamp Stories Anthology.

Burial benefited from the attention of my generous readers John Cayley, Joanna Howard, and C.D. Wright. Sincere thanks to Robert Coover and Brian Evenson for supporting this project. I offer my gratitude to Christian Peet for his belief in this project.

Love to Azareen Van der Vliet Oloomi, whose imagination and good humor inspire me every day. This book would not exist without your desk.

Carl Ferrero, I am grateful for our ongoing collaboration and your assistance in helping me visualize this book.

Many thanks to Patte Loper for contributing artwork for *Burial*'s cover.

David Jhave Johnston, un grand merci for collaborating on the videos. I am thankful for you and your creations.

Bill Hayward, thank you for the author photograph, and for advocating innovative women's writing.

Jeff T. Johnson, thank you for your patience, encouragement, and edits across dozens of drafts. *Let us go then / you and I / and try to unlearn / and put a record on the gramophone.*

To my parents, Rick and Elisabeth, thanks for everything. Je vous aime.

My thinking before, during, and after the process of writing *Burial* was shaped by the following texts and contexts: Virginia Woolf's *The Waves*; Marie Redonnet's *Hôtel Splendid*, *Forever Valley*, and *Rose Mellie Rose*; Clarice Lispector's oeuvre; Tarjei Vesaas's *The Ice Palace*; Hélène Cixous's *Hyperdream* and *The Third Body*; Marguerite Duras's *The Malady of Death*; Rosmarie Waldrop's *Curves to the Apple*; Magdalena Tulli's *Dreams and Stones*; Shelley Jackson's *The Melancholy of Anatomy*; Gaston Bachelard's *The Poetics of Space*; Olivier Rolin's *Hotel Crystal*; Nathalie Sarraute's *The Planetarium*; Deleuze and Guattari's *A Thousand Plateaus*; Ted Mooney's *Easy Travel to Other Planets*; Mina Loy's *The Last Lunar Baedaker*; Alain Robbe-Grillet's *Jealousy*; Lyn Hejinian's *My Life*; Claudia Rankine's *Don't Let Me Be Lonely*; Alain Resnais's *Last Year at Marienbad*; Věra Chytilová's *Daisies*; David Lynch's *Twin Peaks*; Agnès Varda's *The Gleaners and I*; Joanna Newsom's opuses; and Sean McCann's sound environments, to which I edited this book.

ABOUT THE AUTHOR

Claire Donato lives in Brooklyn, NY and writes across genres. She grew up in Pittsburgh, PA and holds an MFA in Literary Arts from Brown University. Her fiction, poetry, and lyric essays have appeared or are forthcoming in the *Boston Review*, *Encyclopedia*, *Evening Will Come*, *LIT*, *Octopus*, and *1913: a journal of forms*. She is the author of a poetry chapbook, *Someone Else's Body* (Cannibal Books) and was a finalist for the National Poetry Series. She has taught at Fordham University, Brown University, The New School, and 826 Valencia/NYC. For more information, visit www. somanytumbleweeds.com.

TARPAULIN SKY PRESS
Current & Forthcoming Titles

FULL-LENGTH BOOKS

CHAPBOOKS

Sandy Florian, *32 Pedals and 47 Stops*

James Haug, *Scratch*

Claire Hero, *Dollyland*

Paula Koneazny, *Installation*

Paul McCormick, *The Exotic Moods of Les Baxter*

Teresa K. Miller, *Forever No Lo*

Jeanne Morel, *That Crossing Is Not Automatic*

Andrew Michael Roberts, *Give Up*

Brandon Shimoda, *The Inland Sea*

Chad Sweeney, *A Mirror to Shatter the Hammer*

Emily Toder, *Brushes With*

G.C. Waldrep, *One Way No Exit*

&

Tarpaulin Sky Literary Journal
in print and online

www.tarpaulinsky.com